By Christine Economos
Illustrated by Lane Gregory

Copyright © 2000 Metropolitan Teaching and Learning Company.
Published by Metropolitan Teaching and Learning Company.
Printed in the United States of America.
All rights reserved. No part of this publication may be reproduced or utilized in any form or by any means, electronic or mechanical, including photocopying, recording, or by any information storage or retrieval system without permission in writing from the publisher. For information regarding permission, write to Metropolitan Teaching and Learning Company, 33 Irving Place, New York, NY 10003.

ISBN 1-58120-030-7

2 3 4 5 6 7 8 9 CL 02 01 00

Marta said, "Do you know what brave little Boo did?
He got a bug and gave it to me."

Ben said, "Mop can grab a pop up, so there!"

Ben said, "We have to brag about them a little.
Our pets are fun and they do a lot."

Ben said, "Mom has pets at her job. She has dogs, cats, mice, and more. See if your grandmother will take us."

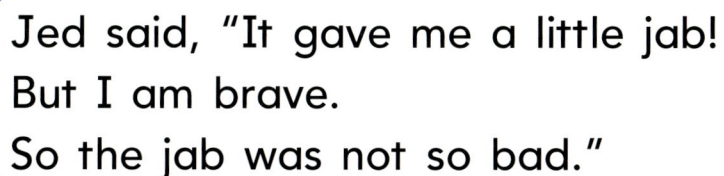

Jed said, "It gave me a little jab!
But I am brave.
So the jab was not so bad."

Jed said, "I will play with my crab.
I will feed it and give it water.
I will get a new shell for it when it grows."